For Amelia and Ellen,
and all the rattletrap trips

P. R.

For Olivia Humphreys and Max Davies,
millennium babies

J. B.

First published 2001 by Walker Books Ltd
87 Vauxhall Walk, London SE11 5HJ

This edition published 2002

2 4 6 8 10 9 7 5 3 1

Text © 2001 Phyllis Root
Illustrations © 2001 Jill Barton

This book has been typeset in Kosmik

Printed in Hong Kong

British Library Cataloguing in Publication Data:
a catalogue record for this book is available from the British Library

ISBN 0-7445-8932-0

THIS WALKER BOOK BELONGS TO:

_____

_____

_____

_____

Rattletrap Car

written by **Phyllis Root** ♦ illustrated by **Jill Barton**

WALKER BOOKS
AND SUBSIDIARIES
LONDON ♦ BOSTON ♦ SYDNEY

Junie was hot.
    Jakie was hot.
  Even the baby was hot hot hot.
   "Let's go to the lake," said
    Junie and Jakie.
  "Go!" said the baby.

"Oh dear," said Dad. "I don't
know if we can make it
in our rattletrap car.
It doesn't go fast and
it doesn't go far."

"Please, please, please!"
cried Junie and Jakie.

"Go!" cried the baby.

"All right," said Dad.
"We'll give it a try."

So he packed up a thermos full of
razzleberry dazzleberry snazzleberry fizz and
some chocolate marshmallow fudge delight.

Junie took her beach-ball.
Jakie took his surf-board.
The baby took her
three-speed,
wind-up,
paddle-wheel boat.

Dad turned the key,
brum brum, brum brum.

Clinkety clankety
bing bang pop!

They were off to the lake
in their rattletrap car.
They didn't go fast and
they didn't go far when ...

boomsssssssss.

The tyre went flat.

"Never mind," said Junie.
"I know just what to do."

She put her beach-ball on the car
and she stuck it on tight with
chocolate marshmallow fudge delight.

Dad turned the key,
brum brum, brum brum.

Lumpety bumpety
clinkety clankety
bing bang pop!

They were off to the lake
in their rattletrap car.
They didn't go fast and
they didn't go far when ...

Whumpety whomp!

The floor fell out.

"Never mind," said Jakie.
"I know just what to do."

He put his surf-board on the car
and he stuck it on tight with
chocolate marshmallow
fudge delight.

Dad turned the key,
brum brum, brum brum.

Wappity bappity
lumpety bumpety
clinkety clankety
bing bang pop!

They were off to the lake
in their rattletrap car.
They didn't go fast and
they didn't go far
when ...

spitter spitter sput!

The petrol tank fell off.

"Never mind," said Dad.
"I know just what to do."

He put the thermos full of razzleberry
dazzleberry snazzleberry fizz on the car
and he stuck it on tight with
chocolate marshmallow fudge delight.

Dad turned the key,
brum brum, brum brum.

Fizzelly sizzelly
wappity bappity
lumpety bumpety
clinkety clankety
bing bang pop!

They were off to
the lake in their
rattletrap car.

They didn't go fast and
they didn't go far when ...

thunketa
thunk!

The engine fell out.

"Oh dear," said Jakie.

"Oh dear," said Junie.

"Oh dear," said Dad.

"Oh dear, oh dear, oh dear, oh dear."

There they sat by the side of the road,
all broken down and hot hot hot,
almost to the lake in their
rattletrap car.

Junie shook her head.
Jakie shook his head.
Dad shook his head.
The baby shook her
three-speed, wind-up,
paddle-wheel boat.

"Go," said the baby.
"Go, go, go."

"Do you think ..." said Junie,
"that it just ..." said Jakie,
"might work?" said Dad.
"Go!" said the baby.

So they took the baby's boat
and put it on the car
and stuck it on tight
with chocolate marshmallow
fudge delight.

Dad turned the key,
brum brum, brum brum.

Flippita fluppita

fizzelly sizzelly

wappity bappity

lumpety bumpety

clinkety clankety

bing bang

pop!

They were off to the lake in their rattletrap car!

They didn't go fast, but they did go far.
They made it to the lake in their rattletrap car!

Junie was cool. Jakie was cool.
Dad and the baby were cool cool cool.
All day long they were cool at the lake
till the sun went down ...

till the moon came up,
and they went

flippita fluppita
fizzelly sizzelly
wappity bappity
lumpety bumpety
clinkety clankety
bing bang pop!

All the way back home.